EAGER LITTLE BEAVER

Joan Stimson

Illustrated by Meg Rutherford

Hippo

EAGER
LITTLE
BEAVER

Scholastic Children's Books
Commonwealth House, 1-19 New Oxford Street,
London WC1A 1NU, UK
a division of Scholastic Ltd
London ~ New York ~ Toronto ~ Sydney ~ Auckland
Mexico City ~ New Delhi ~ Hong Kong

First published in hardback by Scholastic Ltd, 2001
This paperback edition published by Scholastic Ltd, 2002

Text copyright © Joan Stimson, 2001
Illustrations copyright © Meg Rutherford, 2001

ISBN 0 439 99486 1

Printed and bound in China
All rights reserved

2 4 6 8 10 9 7 5 3 1

Once upon a time there was a
beaver called Biff. He lived on
a lake in a house called a lodge.

And never before was a beaver so
much loved, or so well cared for.
Each day Biff went out and about.
Each night he slept safely inside.

"What a contented little beaver," thought Biff's mum and dad.

But one day he took them
both by surprise.
"I don't want to be a beaver,"
said Biff. "I want to be
something exciting instead."

That morning Biff went
in search of adventure.

Before long, a giant
dragonfly appeared.
She zoomed low and
she zigzagged high.

The dragonfly was
an expert flyer.
"That's what I want
to be!" cried Biff.

And, with flapping paws,
he leapt from a rocky ledge.
But Biff splash-landed,
almost before take-off.

"Never mind," said Mum.
"Flying is for insects and birds.
Let's play hide and seek instead."

And that's what they did – in an eager, beavery sort of way.

Next day Biff set off again on his own.
Before long, a large swan appeared.
On her back were three beeping cygnets.
"Look at us," they seemed to say.
"This trip is terrific."
"That's what I want to be!" cried Biff.
And, with strong strokes, he swam
towards the cygnets.

But Mother Swan wouldn't
let Biff on board.

"Never mind," said Dad.
"Swan rides are for baby swans.
Let's go exploring instead."
And that's what they did — in
an eager, beavery sort of way.

A few nights later Biff couldn't get to sleep. For a while he lay awake in the lodge and listened.

Before long, a bear cried out.
And another one answered. The bears
sounded daring and different.
"That's what I want to be!" cried Biff.
And with a quivery shiver, he set off
in search of the noise.

But, when he found the bears,
Biff was scared.
"Never mind," said Mum.
"Those bears should be in bed," said
Dad. And they all snuggled together –
in an eager, beavery sort of way.

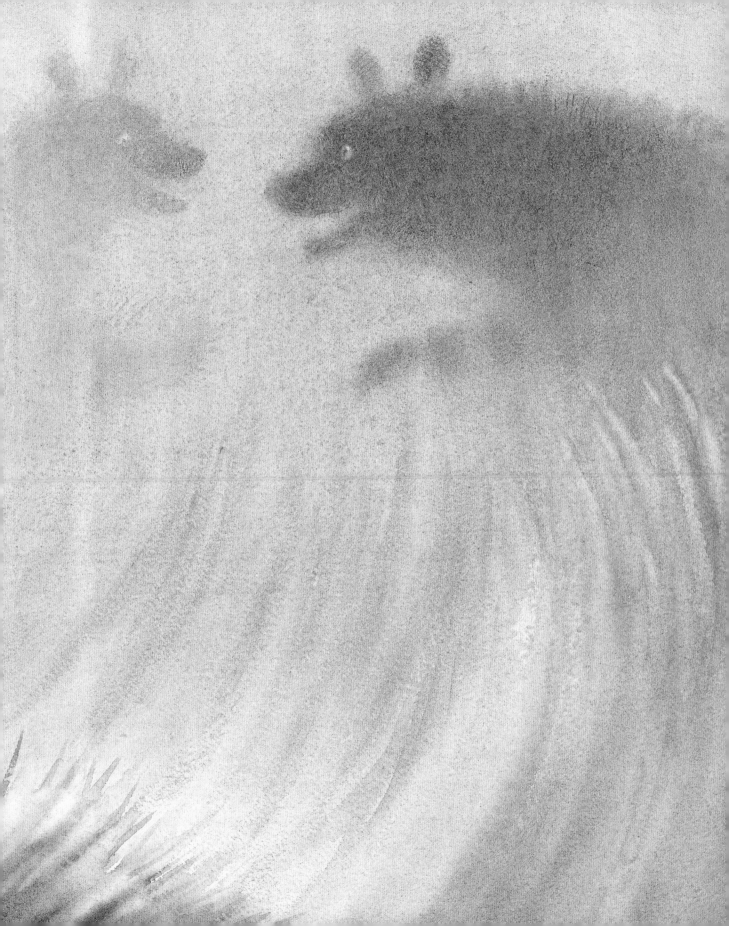

For a whole week
Biff was simply himself.
He began to enjoy
being a beaver.

But late one evening
things went badly wrong.

All through the night, a wild wind howled.
Cruel rain lashed against the lodge.

Next morning Biff crept anxiously outside.
"It's no good being a beaver," he wailed,
"if your house has fallen down."
"Never mind," said Dad.
"It's not as bad as it looks," said Mum.

And together they set to work.
At first Biff watched and worried.
But suddenly, he couldn't sit still.
"I think this twig fits better here,"
said Biff.

From then on, there was no
stopping him. He gnawed and he
clawed. He nudged and he nibbled.
Biff was a natural-born builder!

By the end of the day the lodge was
safer than ever. Biff was exhausted,
but relieved.
"Everything's the same as before,"
he beamed, "only better."

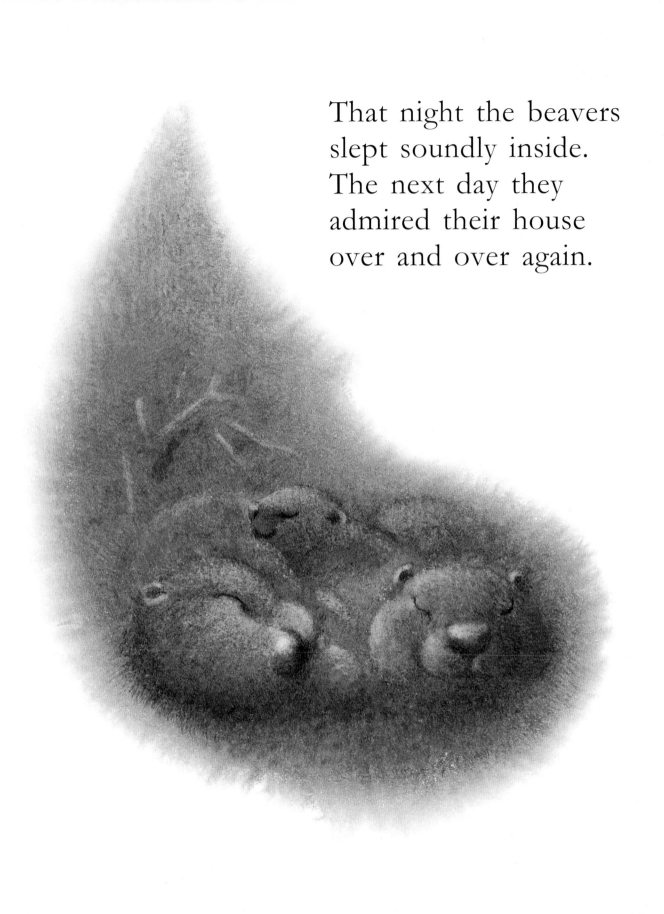

That night the beavers
slept soundly inside.
The next day they
admired their house
over and over again.

And when they
went out and about,
Biff shouted at the
top of his voice,

"IT'S GREAT TO
BE A BEAVER!"

Then he splashed past his parents and raced across the lake – in an eager, beavery sort of way.